Butterflies and Moths

Sally Cowan

Contents

What Are Butterflies and Moths? 2
The Life Cycle of Butterflies and Moths . . 6
Where Butterflies and Moths Live 8
What Butterflies and Moths Eat 10
Clever Camouflage 12
Special Kinds of Butterflies and Moths . . 16
Butterflies, Moths and People 20
Glossary 23
Index 24

What Are Butterflies and Moths?

Butterflies and moths are flying insects.
They are alike in several ways,
but they have some differences.

These creatures all have four wings.
Butterflies' wings are usually bright and colourful.
Most moths have dull grey or brown wings.

butterfly

moth

When butterflies are resting,
they hold their wings up above their backs.
Moths spread their wings out flat when they rest.

Butterflies are active during the daytime,
while most moths are active at night.

butterfly

moth

Butterflies and moths have three main body parts: the head, the thorax and the abdomen. They have six legs, two **antennae** (say: *an-ten-ee*) and two **compound eyes**.

Most butterflies and moths have long, hollow tongues, which they keep rolled up under their heads.

Their wings are covered in tiny scales. The scales can be very colourful. The different colours make patterns on the wings.

This butterfly has its tongue rolled up under its head.

Tiny scales on the wings of a butterfly make patterns.

Differences Between Butterflies and Moths

Butterflies	Moths
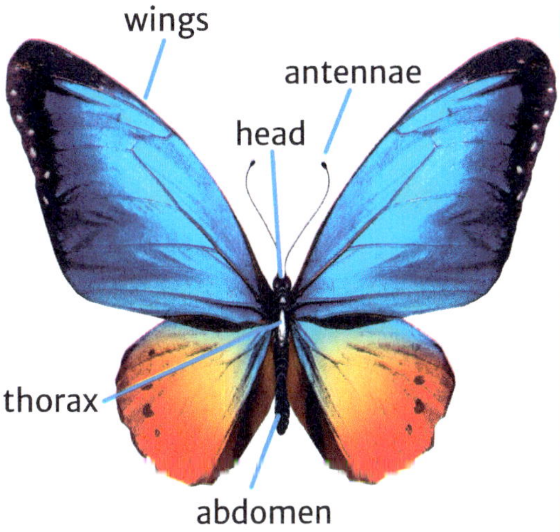 wings antennae head thorax abdomen	 antennae head wings thorax abdomen
active during the day	mostly active at night
bright, colourful wings	dull brown or grey wings
wings upright and together when resting	wings flat when resting
thin antennae with a tiny bump on each end	feathery antennae
thin body	thick body

The Life Cycle of Butterflies and Moths

Butterflies and moths have the same life cycle.
There are four **stages** in the cycle.

The females lay their eggs on plants.
Soon afterwards, tiny caterpillars hatch from the eggs and feast on the plants.

When a caterpillar has eaten enough food, it makes a hard case around its body.
This case is called a pupa (say: *pyoo-pa*).

Inside the pupa, the caterpillar changes into a butterfly or moth.

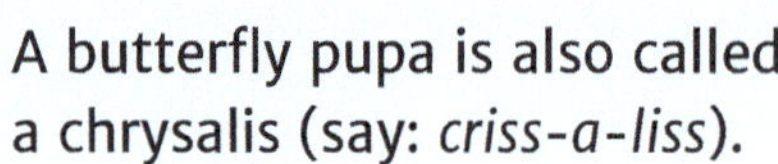

A butterfly pupa is also called a chrysalis (say: *criss-a-liss*).

The Life Cycle of a Painted Lady Butterfly

Where Butterflies and Moths Live

Butterflies and moths live in most places around the world, wherever there are plants.

They live in many different **habitats**, including grasslands, forests, wetlands, parks and gardens.

The ruby-spotted swallowtail butterfly lives in forests and gardens.

The emperor moth lives in grasslands.

Some kinds of butterflies and moths live in places with very cold or hot weather, such as mountains or deserts.

The blue argus butterfly can survive in cold weather.

What Butterflies and Moths Eat

Butterflies and moths cannot eat solid food.
Most of them sip the **nectar** from flowers.
When they land on a flower, they unroll their tongues and suck up the nectar.

Butterflies and moths do not taste with their tongues. They taste with their feet.

There are some kinds of moths that do not eat at all because they have no mouthparts.
They live off the food they ate when they were hungry caterpillars.
These moths only live long enough to breed and lay eggs.

Luna caterpillars eat a lot before they become moths.

an adult luna moth

The luna moth has no mouthparts.

Clever Camouflage

Butterflies and moths are a tasty meal for birds, spiders and other small animals.
But many butterflies and moths have **camouflage**. This helps to protect them from these predators.

There are butterflies that look like dead leaves and butterflies that blend into the plants they feed on.

The wings of the Indian leaf butterfly look like dead leaves.

The glasswing butterfly has see-through wings.
It can be difficult for predators to see this butterfly.

The pupa of the glasswing butterfly
looks like a drop of water glistening in the sunshine.

a glasswing butterfly

a glasswing butterfly pupa

Some moths blend easily into tree trunks or leaves.
This is important camouflage
because most moths rest in the daytime.
Hungry predators cannot see the moths.

Owl moths have two big spots on their wings
that look like the eyes of an owl.
Many birds and reptiles are scared of owls,
so they stay away from this moth.

Moth caterpillars have camouflage, too.
Many caterpillars are the same colour
as the green leaves they feed on.
Others look like small twigs growing on a plant.

Pepper moth caterpillars have camouflage that helps them look like twigs.

Special Kinds of Butterflies and Moths

Some kinds of butterflies and moths
are very special.
They live in different parts of the world.

The Queen Alexandra's birdwing butterfly
lives in rainforest in Papua New Guinea.
It is the largest butterfly in the world,
with a **wingspan** of about 28 centimetres.

The wingspan of the Queen Alexandra's birdwing butterfly is almost the same length as a school ruler.

The yellow admiral butterfly is a very strong flier. These small butterflies can travel over the sea between Australia and New Zealand.

The zebra swallowtail butterfly lives in North America. It has black and white stripes, and long tails on its back wings.

The Hercules moth lives in rainforests in northern Australia and the island of New Guinea. It has the largest wings of all moths, with a wingspan of 27 centimetres. The Hercules moth can only live for a short time, because it has no mouthparts and cannot eat.

Male Hercules moths have long tails on their back wings.

The hummingbird hawkmoth is a small moth that lives in many places around the world. During the daytime, it hovers close to flowers as it sips nectar with its long tongue. It can fly very fast to escape predators.

The hummingbird hawkmoth can hover like a hummingbird.

Butterflies, Moths and People

Wherever there are plenty of butterflies and moths, scientists know that the environment is healthy.

Butterflies and moths spread **pollen**
as they feed on flowers.
This helps fruits and vegetables to grow.
Animals and people eat these foods.

Butterflies and moths are also food for many animals, such as birds and spiders.

For hundreds of years, people have kept silkworm caterpillars because they spin beautiful silk threads.

But people often think of caterpillars as pests that eat holes in plants or in people's clothing. Sometimes, **toxic** sprays are used to kill the caterpillars.

Silkworm caterpillars spin silk threads.

The habitats of many butterflies and moths are being destroyed by people. Large areas of grassland and forest have been cleared for building houses or farms.

People need to share the environment with butterflies and moths. These small creatures are an important part of life on Earth.

Glossary

antennae (*noun*) feelers or stalks on an insect's head

camouflage (*noun*) colours or patterns that help an animal blend into a background

compound eyes (*noun*) eyes that are made up of different parts that work separately

habitats (*noun*) places where animals usually live

nectar (*noun*) a sweet liquid made by flowers

pollen (*noun*) the powder that is found inside flowers, which helps to make new seeds

stages (*noun*) the separate parts of a process

toxic (*adjective*) poisonous to animals or plants

wingspan (*noun*) the measurement across both wings when they are spread out flat

Index

antennae 4, 5, 23

Australia 17, 18

camouflage 12–15, 23

caterpillars 6, 7, 11, 15, 21

eggs 6, 7, 11

glasswing butterfly 13

habitats 8–9, 16, 17, 18, 19, 22, 23

Hercules moth 18

hummingbird hawkmoth 19

life cycle 6–7

luna moth 11

mouthparts 11, 18

nectar 10, 19, 23

New Guinea 18

New Zealand 17

North America 17

painted lady butterfly 7

Papua New Guinea 16

predators 12, 13, 14, 19, 20

pupa 6, 7, 13

Queen Alexandra's birdwing butterfly 16

scales 4

silkworm caterpillars 21

wings 2, 3, 4, 5, 13, 14, 16, 17, 18, 23

yellow admiral butterfly 17

zebra swallowtail butterfly 17